Laura Ingalls Wilder

MY FIRST LITTLE HOUSE BOOKS

GOING

TO

TOWN

ADAPTED FROM THE LITTLE HOUSE BOOKS

By Laura Ingalls Wilder

Illustrated by Renée Graef

HARPERCOLLINS PUBLISHERS

For my Mom, Louise
—R.G.

Going to Town Text adapted from Little House in the Big Woods, copyright 1932, 1960 Little House Heritage Trust.
Illustrations copyright © 1995 by Renée Graef. *Manufactured in China.* All rights reserved. Library of Congress
Cataloging-in-Publication Data Wilder, Laura Ingalls, 1867–1957. Going to town / by Laura Ingalls Wilder;
illustrated by Renée Graef. p. cm.—(My first little house books) "A little house book." Summary: A little
pioneer girl and her family, living in the Big Woods of Wisconsin, make their first trip into town to visit the general store.
ISBN 0-06-443452-4 (pbk.) [1. Frontier and pioneer life—Wisconsin—Fiction. 2. Family life—Wisconsin—Fiction.
3. Wisconsin—Fiction.] I. Graef, Renée, ill. II. Title. III. Series. PZ7.W6461Go 1995 E—dc20 92-46722
CIP AC HarperCollins®, ■®, and Little House® are trademarks of HarperCollins Publishers Inc.
Visit us on the World Wide Web! www.littlehousebooks.com
For information address HarperCollins Children's Books, a division of HarperCollins Publishers,
195 Broadway, New York, NY 10007.
15 16 SCP 20 19 18 17

Illustrations for the My First Little House Books are inspired by the work of Garth Williams with his permission, which we gratefully acknowledge.

Once upon a time, a little girl named Laura lived in the Big Woods of Wisconsin in a little house made of logs.

She lived in the little house with her Pa, her Ma, her big sister Mary, her baby sister Carrie, and their good old bulldog Jack.

One day Pa said that as soon as he had finished planting the crops, they would all go to town. Laura, Mary, and Carrie could go too. They were old enough now.

Laura and Mary were very excited! The next day they tried to play going to town. They could not do it very well, because they were not sure what a town was like. They had never even seen a store.

Then one night Pa said, "We'll go to town tomorrow." That night Ma gave Laura and Mary a bath. Then she wound their wet hair tightly on lots of little rags. In the morning their hair would be curly.

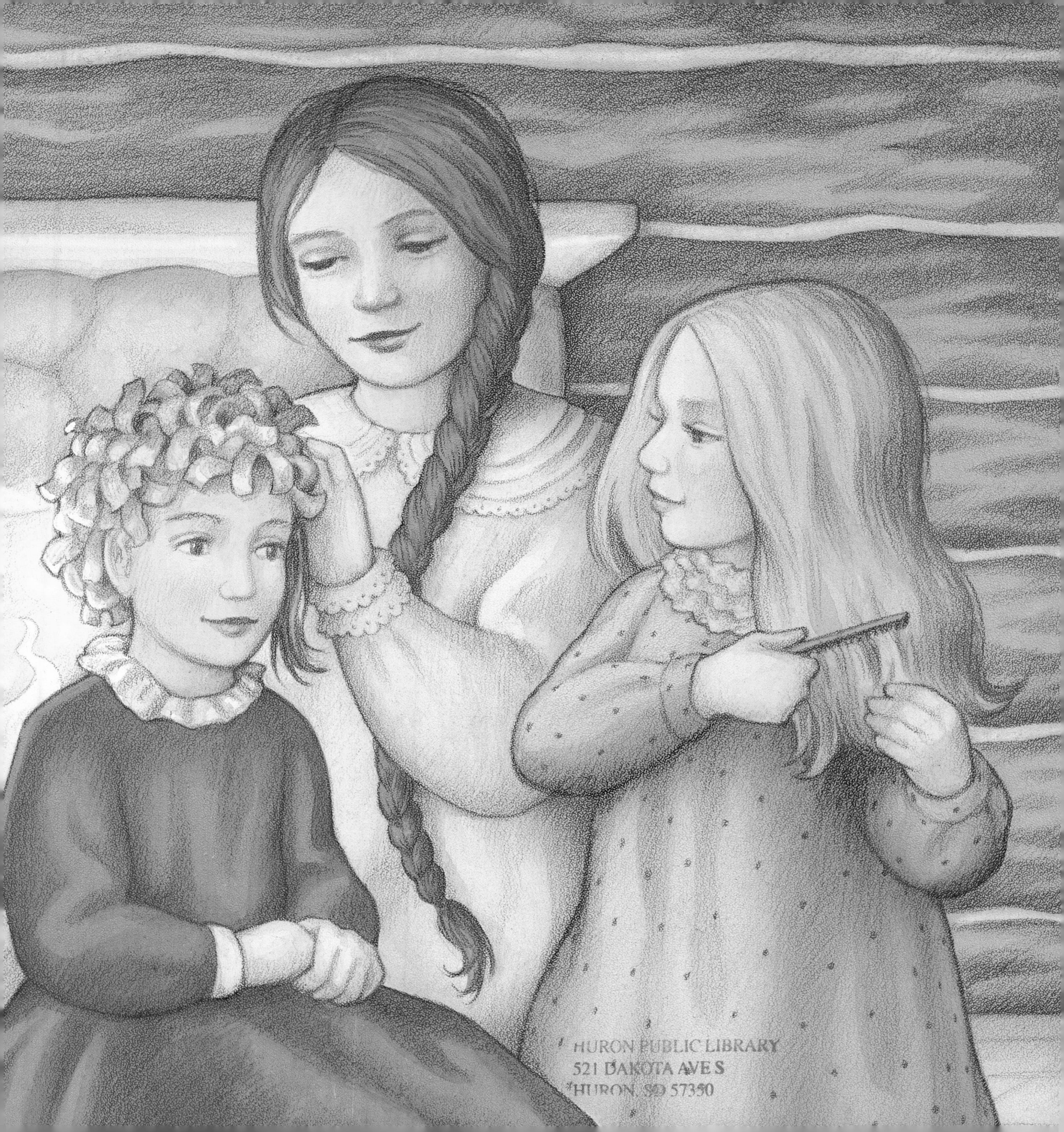

When Laura and Mary woke up, they put on their best dresses. Mary buttoned up the back of Laura's red calico dress, and Ma buttoned up the back of Mary's blue calico dress. Then Ma took the rags out of their hair and combed it into long round curls that hung down over their shoulders.

After breakfast Pa drove the wagon up to the gate of the little house. He had brushed the horses until they shone. Ma sat up on the wagon seat with Pa, holding Baby Carrie in her arms. Laura and Mary sat behind Ma and Pa on a board across the wagon box. They were going to town!

They were happy as they rode through the springtime woods. Ma was smiling, Carrie laughed and bounced, and Pa whistled while he drove the horses. Rabbits stood up in the road ahead, and the sun shone through their tall ears. Twice Laura and Mary saw deer looking at them with their large, dark eyes among the trees.

Suddenly Pa stopped the horses and pointed ahead with his whip. "There you are, Laura and Mary!" he said. "There's the town of Pepin."

Laura had never imagined so many houses and so many people. There were more houses than she could count. Laura looked and looked, and could not say a word.

Pa helped everyone down from the wagon, and they walked up to the biggest building in town. This was the store where Pa came to trade. As they climbed up the steps of the store, Laura was so excited that she was trembling all over.

The store was full of things to look at. There were sacks of salt and sugar. There were pink and blue and red and brown and purple fabrics for dresses. There were boots and hammers and nails and big wooden pails full of candy. There were so many things that Laura did not know how Pa and Ma could ever choose.

When all the trading was done, the storekeeper gave Mary and Laura each a piece of candy. They were so surprised that they just stood looking at their candies. Then they remembered and said, "Thank you." The candies were shaped like hearts and had printing on them. Mary's candy said:

> *Roses are red,*
> *Violets are blue,*
> *Sugar is sweet,*
> *And so are you.*

Laura's said only:

> *Sweets to the sweet.*

After they left the store, they walked over to the lake at the edge of town. They all sat on the warm sand, and Ma opened the picnic basket that she had brought. Inside there were bread and butter and cheese, hard-boiled eggs, and cookies for lunch.

After the picnic was over, they all got back into the wagon to go home. It was a long trip through the Big Woods to the little house. Laura and Mary were very tired, and Baby Carrie was asleep in Ma's arms. But Pa sang softly:

"'Mid pleasures and palaces, though we may roam,
Be it ever so humble, there's no place like home."